Princess Ponies

A Singing Star

With special thanks to Julie Sykes

Bloomsbury Publishing, London, New Delhi, New York and Sydney

First published in Great Britain in May 2014 by Bloomsbury Publishing Plc
50 Bedford Square, London WC1B 3DP

www.bloomsbury.com
www.ChloeRyder.com

Bloomsbury is a trademark of Bloomsbury Publishing Plc

Text copyright © Awesome Media and Entertainment Ltd 2014
Illustrations copyright © Jennifer Miles 2014

The moral rights of the author and illustrator have been asserted

A CIP catalogue record for this book is available from the British Library

ISBN 978 1 4088 5421 1

Typeset by Hewer Text UK Ltd, Edinburgh
Printed and bound in Great Britain by CPI Group (UK) Ltd, Croydon CR0 4YY

3 5 7 9 10 8 6 4 2

Princess Ponies

A Singing Star

CHLOE RYDER

Illustrated by Jennifer Miles

BLOOMSBURY

LONDON NEW DELHI NEW YORK SYDNEY

The Pony

Queen
Moonshine

Princess
Crystal

Princess
Cloud

Princess
Stardust

Princess
Honey

Royal Family

King
Firestar

Prince
Jet

Prince
Comet

Prince
Storm

Chevalia

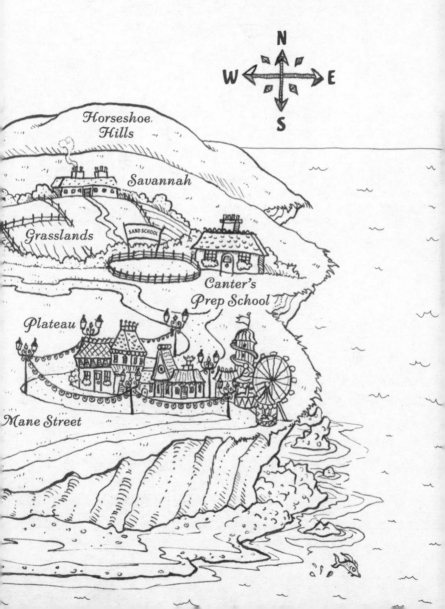

In the middle of the Horseshoe Hills, far away from the Royal Court and Stableside Castle, lay the ruins of a smaller castle. Its crumbling walls were choked with ivy. Bats flew from the turrets and spiders scuttled along the empty passageways.

In a damp room at the back of the castle, a chestnut pony with bulging eyes and a square nose, wearing a dark cloak, was bent over a glass container supported above a small fire. A gooey liquid, thicker than syrup, bubbled fiercely in the container, sending clouds of black smoke swirling into the air. The pony's eyes watered and she coughed violently. She buried her nose in her cloak until the smoke thinned.

'At last it is ready.' Divine, the pony, carefully lifted the container away from the fire with a pair of tongs and carried it over to a sturdy oak table. She watched as the bubbles settled and then, when the liquid was still, she poured it into a bottle and sealed it with a cork.

Divine spoke softly at first. 'No one understands me. All I ever wanted was for the ponies of Chevalia to love me. And soon they will.' She held the bottle

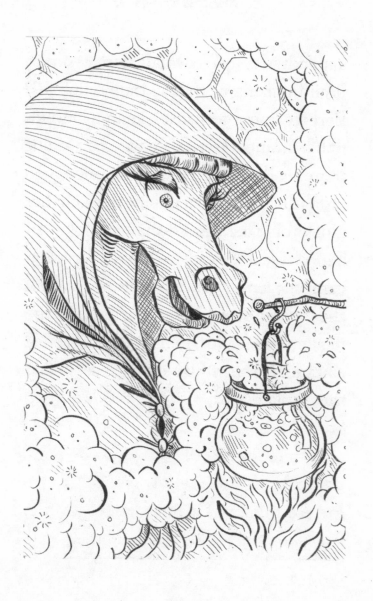

up and her lips curved into a smile. 'With this magic potion the ponies will all love me the most. Then Chevalia will be mine!' Her voice rose to a shout and ended with a cackling laugh.

With great care Divine tucked the bottle of black liquid into a pocket of her cloak. She turned to a cracked mirror hanging from a nail on the wall and pulled up her hood, arranging the material to cover her face. 'Ponies of Chevalia,' she whispered, 'fear not. I have a plan!'

Chapter 1

Pippa MacDonald was helping her mum set up a picnic in the riverside park. It was a bright, warm Sunday afternoon, but Pippa's mind was elsewhere.

'I need to rehearse my lines for the school play,' said Pippa. She reached over to the picnic hamper and picked up her script. 'Can you help me, Mum?'

'No, no,' said Jack, Pippa's little brother. 'Mum said she'd play football with me, didn't you, Mum?'

Pippa sighed. Jack was always begging for Mum's attention. 'I did promise Jack I'd play with him,' she said. 'But I expect Miranda will listen to you.'

Miranda looked up from her book. 'Do I have to?'

'You could play football with your brother instead,' offered Pippa's mum.

'Not much of a choice,' huffed Miranda. 'Come on, Pip, let's find somewhere quiet to practise your lines where we won't get hit by Jack's football.'

'Great,' Pippa handed Miranda the play script. 'We could go under that big tree, away from the river.'

Miranda sat under the tree and stared at Pippa from over the top of the script.

Pippa's stomach knotted and she shoved her hands in her pockets.

'Stand up straight,' Miranda said, bossily. 'It says here that you're a knight but right now you look more like a sack of dried pasta.'

Pippa flushed as she took her hands out of her pockets and pushed her shoulders back.

'Better,' said Miranda. 'Go on then, say something.'

'Um . . .' For one heart-stopping moment Pippa couldn't remember her lines.

'Dragons,' prompted Miranda.

Dragons, of course! In a rush Pippa said, 'I will fight the dragon. Bring me my armour, and Jasper, go and saddle my horse.'

'Slower,' bellowed Miranda, 'and much louder. I can hardly hear you.'

Pippa's face burned with embarrassment. She started again but she was so self-conscious that she muddled up her words.

'Stop!' Miranda cut her off with a wave of her hand. 'You sound like a little mouse. Do it again, but more like a dragon this time.'

Pippa tried again but with Miranda's bossy comments ringing in her ears she couldn't concentrate. Almost every time she spoke she either forgot her lines or she wasn't loud enough. Her heart sank. She wondered if maybe she should stick to riding ponies instead of acting.

'Go on, Pippa, you can do it.' Mum ran past, chasing a football. 'It's like riding a pony – you just need to practise.'

'I am practising and it isn't working,' Pippa said, desperately.

Mum ran back. 'You need to practise some more then. And more importantly you need to believe in yourself. You *can* do it.'

As Mum went back to the game of football, Miranda held up the script. 'Is there any point in trying again?' she asked.

Pippa shook her head. She felt hopeless at acting. 'I think I'll have a rest,' she said. Biting back the tears welling in her eyes, Pippa wandered over to the river. As she stared into the blue-green water she thought how her best Princess Pony friend, Stardust, would never tease her for not being good at something. But she couldn't tell Miranda that. She'd never believe her.

Stardust, and her magical home of

Chevalia, was her special secret. A month ago, on Pippa's seaside holiday, two giant seahorses had taken her to Chevalia, an island where Royal Ponies reigned. Chevalia had been in danger but Pippa and Stardust had saved it by finding eight golden horseshoes. The horseshoes had been stolen from a wall in the ancient Stableside Castle by a mean-spirited pony who was called Baroness Divine. Divine had escaped but, with the horseshoes back in their rightful place, the Princess Ponies felt safe again.

The bulrushes growing in the water rustled and began to sway and suddenly a pink, horse-like head with large, round eyes popped up.

'Rosella?' Pippa blinked. She couldn't believe that one moment she had been daydreaming about Chevalia, and the next moment one of the giant seahorses was right here in front of her. When she looked again the seahorse was still staring back at her.

'Pippa MacDonald,' Rosella bowed

her head. She was carrying a rolled-up scroll, tied with a pink ribbon, around her neck. 'This is for you.'

An icy feeling spread through Pippa. Was there trouble in Chevalia? Her hand trembled as she reached forward to take the scroll.

'Don't worry.' Rosella's dark eyes were kindly. 'It's a royal invitation.'

As Pippa unrolled the scroll, silver musical notes flew into the air and a sweet voice sang out, 'Pippa MacDonald, the King and Queen of Chevalia invite you to a royal performance by the Royal Pony Orchestra, accompanied by Diva, the Duchess of Savannah.'

As the voice faded the invitation appeared in writing on the scroll.

Underneath Stardust had added a note in pink writing. 'Please say you'll come. My cousin Diva has an amazing voice. It's going to be a magical night!'

Pippa smiled. How could the concert not be magical when it was taking place in her beloved Chevalia?

'Yes, please,' she said immediately. 'I'd love to come.'

'Good.' Rosella trod water next to the bank. 'Climb aboard, Pippa. Chevalia awaits you!'

Pippa grasped Rosella's long, pink spines as she climbed on to the seahorse's back.

'Hold on tight,' said Rosella. 'To Chevalia.'

As Rosella swam to the middle of the

river Pippa glanced back at her family. They were frozen like statues. Mum was in mid-run, chasing after the football, and Jack was in the air, halfway through a jump. Miranda was lying on her tummy on the picnic blanket, her nose buried in her book. Pippa waved, even though she knew they couldn't see her. The moment she'd climbed on to Rosella's back she'd entered a magic time bubble. Pippa could stay in Chevalia for as long as she liked but she wouldn't be missed, as no time would pass in her own world.

As Rosella sped down the River Thames, Pippa sat back and enjoyed the sights of London whizzing past and above her: the majestic Houses of Parliament, the massive London Eye, Tower Bridge, and the stern stone walls of the Tower of London. Further on they sailed past the shiny silver Thames flood barrier and into the open countryside until at last they were out on the choppy open sea. Pippa loved riding the waves with Rosella. Her curly hair streamed behind her and she tasted salt on her lips.

Soon they arrived on the shores of a large island. The long, sandy beach was edged with trees.

'Thank you, Rosella.' Pippa patted Rosella's neck as she jumped into the clear, blue water.

'Enjoy the concert,' called Rosella.

As Pippa waded to the shore she wondered how much time it would take her to walk to Stableside Castle.

She'd only ever made the journey on horseback. She stepped through the surf and on to the beach. Something was moving in the trees. Pippa's heart leapt.

'Stardust,' she exclaimed as a pure white pony galloped across the sand.

Chapter 2

'You came!' Princess Stardust's hooves threw up clouds of sand as she stopped a horsehair away from Pippa. She whickered softly and nuzzled Pippa's curly, brown hair.

'Of course,' Pippa threw her arms around Stardust's neck and hugged her friend back. 'I wouldn't have missed the big concert and seeing you again for anything.'

'I can't wait for you to meet my cousin Diva,' said Stardust. 'She's got an amazing voice and she's so much fun to be with. You're going to love her. Jump on my back and I'll take you to her now.'

Pippa put her hands on Stardust's snowy white neck and vaulted aboard. Stardust took off, galloping across the beach and into the Wild Forest. She hurtled through the trees, leaping over the puddles of quick-stick mud. They passed a group of wild ponies playing in a clearing. Pippa waved and the wild ponies stamped their hooves and whinnied back. A short while later Pippa glimpsed the eight turrets of Stableside Castle stretching above the treetops.

The woods thinned and Stardust slowed to a trot as she came out on to a grassy plateau. Pippa turned her head to get a look at Mane Street. Sparkly, star-shaped bunting hung from the lamp posts and the flower beds were bursting with colourful flowers and extra large carrots for the ponies to snack on.

'I've booked us and Diva into the Mane Street Salon for some pampering before the concert,' said Stardust. 'Honey's coming too. Miss Hoofberry has a new glittery hoof polish that she's desperate to try.' Stardust chattered on, filling Pippa in on everything that had happened since they last met. As they took the windy path up to the Castle Stardust said, 'But that's enough about me. What have you been up to?'

Pippa didn't want to admit to her best pony friend that she was nervous about the school play. 'Nothing much. It's been mostly school stuff,' said Pippa.

'Did you tell your school friends about Chevalia?' asked Stardust. 'I bet they are all so envious of you!'

'Well, I wrote a story all about Chevalia and read it out to the whole class. My teacher said I had a brilliant imagination.'

Stardust giggled. 'Didn't anyone believe it?'

'I don't think so,' Pippa said, sadly. 'But I suppose that's a good thing. Chevalia wouldn't be the same if humans found out about it.'

'Still, that was very brave of you to read aloud to the whole class. Didn't you get stage fright?'

Pippa fell silent. She'd been petrified when she'd read her story to the class. Performing in the school play would be even scarier because she'd have to act as well as speak in front of everyone.

She was just gathering her courage to tell Stardust all about it when the pearly white walls of Stableside Castle rose before her and the moment was lost. A group of ponies, with cameras hanging around their necks, were waiting by the drawbridge.

'The ponarazzi have been camped outside the castle there ever since Diva arrived,' Stardust explained. 'There are pictures of her in all the magazines and newspapers.'

'Where are we going?' asked Pippa, as instead of crossing the drawbridge Stardust had trotted around the side of the Castle.

'Just wait and see,' Stardust said, mysteriously.

A few minutes later they arrived at the edge of an enormous amphitheatre. 'Wow!' Pippa stared at the huge, horse-shoe-shaped stage in the centre. 'I never knew this was here.'

'It wasn't — until last week,' said Stardust. 'We'll be over there in the royal box.' She nodded to a box in the middle of the amphitheatre. It was decorated with coloured rosettes and had an amazing view. A group of ponies were gathered on the stage.

'That's Diva, there,' Stardust said, excitedly.

Pippa looked and saw a tall pony with a shiny coat as black as midnight. Her dark eyes shone like jewels and she had a pretty white blaze on her nose.

She was every inch the superstar with her sparkly, pink tiara, her head held high and her ears pricked forward. Her voice wasn't so pretty, though. As they approached Pippa heard her complain, 'Am I supposed to scrub my own carrots? How can I be expected to give my best performance when the food is unwashed?' Diva stamped a hoof to drive home her point. 'And the lighting is all wrong. It's far too dark – no one will be able to see me! And I am the star of the show.'

'How awful!' called Stardust. 'Have you complained to Dad? He'll sort it out for you.'

'Stardust, da . . . ha . . . ling!' Diva swung round and her voice softened.

She trotted over to Stardust and they rubbed noses. 'And you brought your pet girl!' she added.

'Friend,' said Pippa.

'Yes. Diva, meet my best *friend* Pippa. Pippa, this is my hugely talented cousin Diva,' Stardust said, proudly. 'She's the star in the family.'

Pippa slipped from Stardust's back. 'Pleased to meet you, Diva,' she said, shyly.

'Da . . . ha . . . ling. Come here.' Diva blew softly through her nose at Pippa then nuzzled her hair. 'This is soooo exciting. I've been dy . . . hy . . . ing to meet you. I've heard so much about how you saved Chevalia. I'm going to dedicate a special song in the show just to you!'

'That's enough chatter.' A plump pony with a blue rinse in her dark brown mane and tail promptly trotted on to the stage.

'Hello, Aunty Rainbow,' said Stardust. 'I was just introducing Pippa to Diva. Remember Pippa, the girl that found the eight missing horseshoes and saved Chevalia?'

'Yes, yes,' said Rainbow. She tossed her head impatiently. 'And we're all very grateful that you saved the island, but right now I've got a *concert* to save. This is Diva's last rehearsal before the royal performance. It's important we don't distract her. I've invited the ponarazzi in to take some photographs and I've arranged an audience. The ponies from the Mighty Oaks Senior Ponies Stables are here.' She nodded to the lower tiers of the amphitheatre, where a procession of older ponies were slowly taking their seats. The orchestra pit was also filling up with the musicians and their instruments. They all looked very smart, the boys wearing royal red sashes and the girls in silvery pink.

'Can we stay and watch?' asked Stardust.

'As long as you're both quiet as a pair of baby seahorses.' Rainbow turned to Diva. 'Have you done your warm-up scales?'

Stardust whispered to Pippa. 'Let's watch from the wings. I've often wanted to help backstage but Mrs Steeplechase says that it's not a fitting place for a princess.'

Mrs Steeplechase, the royal nanny, was very strict and had old-fashioned ideas about the right way for a Princess Pony to behave. Pippa followed Stardust into the wings and they stood to the side of a huge screen decorated with pictures of Chevalia.

The orchestra finished tuning their instruments. The conductor waved a baton and silence fell in the amphitheatre. Goosebumps marched along Pippa's arms, making her shiver with pleasure. She loved the start of a concert or play, just so long as she wasn't acting in it!

The conductor waved his stick again and the orchestra burst into life. Onstage, Diva took a deep breath, held her head high and began to sing. As her voice rose there was a commotion behind Pippa. A draught of air lifted her hair as someone rushed past her and on to the stage. Pippa gasped. She recognised the cloaked figure galloping towards Diva, who whinnied in fright.

The charging pony was none other than Divine.

A harsh cackle filled the air. There was a loud bang and thick, black smoke curled around Diva's hooves. She shrieked but her scream was cut short. As the smoke cleared Pippa noticed Divine had a glass bottle hanging around her neck, containing a black liquid that sparkled magically.

'Thought the show would go on without me, did you?' Divine's voice rose to a screech. 'Well, think again. Diva can't sing any more. My magic potion has captured her singing voice in this bottle.' Divine's hood fell away as she threw back her head and cackled again. She bucked wildly, kicking her back hooves high in the air, and jumped from the stage. Four guards tried to stop her but Divine dived round them, soared over the gate and galloped into the distance.

An eerie silence filled the arena. It was broken by Diva's sobs. Stardust and Pippa hurried towards the stage but Rainbow got there first. 'Stuff and nonsense,' she said, crossly. 'Start again, Diva, from the beginning. Lights, please.'

34

A spotlight snapped on, encircling Diva in a bright, white light. Diva opened her mouth then shut it again. Her lip trembled. 'I can't,' she whispered.

'Rubbish!' said Rainbow. 'Hurry up. We don't have time to waste.'

Diva shook her head. 'There's no point,' she said. 'I won't be able to sing. Divine has stolen my voice.'

Rainbow stamped her hoof. 'The only thing she has stolen is three minutes of precious rehearsal time. Now sing!'

Diva opened her mouth but no sound came out.

'I can't,' she sobbed. 'My singing voice has gone. I'm just an ordinary pony now.' Diva reared up dramatically then thundered off the stage.

Chapter 3

Stardust stared at Pippa. Her eyes were bright with alarm. 'Poor Diva,' she neighed. 'We have to help her. Jump on my back, Pippa. We'll chase after Divine and get Diva's voice back.'

Pippa hesitated for a moment. Something was bothering her but each time she tried to remember what it was, the thought slipped even deeper into her mind.

'Pippa, hurry!' Stardust tossed her head.

'We ought to go after Diva first,' Pippa said, slowly. 'She was very upset.'

'Oh! I didn't think about that. Yes, we must.'

Stardust barely waited for Pippa to land on her back before she set off at a gallop away from the Castle.

Pippa leaned forward to call in Stardust's ear. 'Where are we going?'

'To Diva's stables.'

'Why would she go there? No one's at home. They'll all be on their way here to Stableside for the concert. And Diva seems like the kind of pony who needs an audience.'

'That's true,' Stardust slowed down.

'Then where would a star go when she's lost her singing voice?'

Pippa thought about it for a moment. 'To her unicorn?' she suggested.

'Of course!' shouted Stardust. 'Pippa MacDonald, you are so clever. I bet she's gone to find her unicorn twin.'

For every pony on Chevalia there was an identical unicorn friend. The unicorns loved to sing and they had beautiful voices. If anyone could understand how Diva was feeling about losing her voice it would be her magical unicorn friend.

Stardust changed direction and cantered towards the Grasslands. Pippa leaned forward, sinking her hands into Stardust's long, silky mane. The wind was behind them – it pushed Stardust along and blew Pippa's curly hair over her face so she could hardly see where they were going. They crossed the Savannah and a while later Stardust slowed to a fast trot. 'We're nearly there,' she whispered.

Pippa sat back. Ahead lay the Cloud Forest, home of the unicorns. Stardust stepped carefully as she entered the mysterious woods, shrouded in mist.

The trees towered over them, making Pippa feel as small as an ant. They hadn't gone far when Pippa saw something moving ahead of them.

'There she is,' Pippa said.

Diva trotted deeper into the forest.

'Diva, wait,' called Pippa.

Diva was far ahead and didn't seem to hear. Stardust hurried on. A low mist swirled around Pippa and Stardust's legs so it looked like they were floating across a milky white lake. The ancient trees were hung with thick, rope-like vines and Pippa and Stardust had to push together to move them out of their way.

A dragonfly swooped overhead – its electric blue wings beat rapidly and long, red flames of fire shot from its mouth. Stardust stood very still and the dragonfly ignored her and flew on. The ground grew spongier. Water squelched around Stardust's hooves.

'Shall I walk?' offered Pippa, as Stardust's hooves sank deep into the ground.

'*Shhh.*' Stardust stopped suddenly. Her ears swivelled forward and began to twitch. 'Can you hear that?'

Pippa's lips curled into a smile. 'Singing,' she said. 'It's so beautiful.'

Stardust walked on towards the sound of the music. She went around the trunk of a huge tree with massive green leaves and waited. They'd reached a clearing and there was Diva, listening to a small unicorn sing.

The unicorn was almost identical to Diva. She had a jet-black coat with a flowing, black mane and tail and a white blaze on her nose. She was much smaller than Diva and had a silver horn in the middle of her forehead.

Her voice was sweeter than a night-ingale's. She stopped singing as Stardust approached and curtsied so low that her long, black mane swept across the forest floor. 'Princess Stardust, and Pippa, the human girl. What a wonderful surprise. My name is Harmony.'

'Thank you, Harmony. It's lovely to see you too.' Stardust curtsied back and Pippa slid to the ground and curtsied alongside her.

Diva hung her head low, barely looking up to see Pippa and Stardust. She looked terribly upset.

'Did you hear what happened?' Stardust asked. 'Now that Diva's lost her singing voice there won't be a royal concert tonight.'

Harmony nodded. 'Diva's just told me how Divine stole it.'

'There won't be a concert,' whispered Diva. 'Not tonight, not ever.'

Harmony smiled. 'But if you still have your speaking voice, Diva, then you'll be able to sing.'

'I can't.' Two large tears welled in Diva's eyes and ran down her face. 'My speaking voice can't possibly be anything to do with my singing voice. It's far too ordinary.' Her voice dropped to an ashamed whisper. 'It would be too embarrassing to sing with my normal speaking voice.'

'It sounds to me that it's not your singing voice that's gone,' said Harmony, 'but your confidence.'

A memory sparked in Pippa's head. The thing that had been bugging her earlier, it was something that Mum had shouted to her when she was rehearsing her lines with Miranda. What was it? Suddenly it came to her. 'You can do it, Diva,' she said. 'You just have to practise and you have to believe in yourself.'

Diva stood stiffly with her front hooves crossed. 'No,' she said. 'Unless Divine gives me my voice back I'll never sing again.'

A loud buzzing sounded overhead and a horsefly flew into the clearing. He hovered just in front of Pippa's face. 'What'sss going on?' he asked. 'When did the concert get moved?'

'Zimb!' cried Pippa in delight. She'd been friends with Zimb since he'd

helped find two of the missing gold horseshoes in the Grasslands. 'The concert is at Stableside Castle, only it might not go ahead now. Divine has stolen Diva's singing voice.'

'That'sss terrible,' buzzed Zimb, darting around in the air.

47

Something was puzzling Pippa. 'Why did you think the concert had been moved?' she asked.

'Well,' said Zimb, 'I was flying near the coastline when I heard shouting in the Echo Caves, ssso I went inside to sssee if anyone needed help. I sssearched the tunnelsss in the caves until I found Divine with a ssstrange glass bottle around her neck. She was talking to herself about how she'd taken away something more important than Diva's voice. I knew something wasn't right so I flew to Ssstableside Castle to warn Diva, but on my way I sssaw you and Stardust trot into the Cloud Foressst. I think Divine is up to no good.'

'That's for certain,' Pippa said, thinking about what to do next. 'Where are the Echo Caves?'

'Not far from here,' said Stardust.

'Can we go and get my singing voice back?' asked Diva.

A look passed between Stardust and Pippa.

'Of course we can,' said Pippa.

Stardust lowered herself for Pippa to climb on. 'We'll be faster if you ride.'

Pippa jumped on to Stardust's back.

'Where are you going?' asked Zimb.

'To the Echo Caves,' said Pippa. 'To rescue Diva's singing voice.'

Chapter 4

'I'll come too,' said Harmony. 'Follow me and I'll show you a quick way through the Cloud Forest.'

Harmony took off at a gallop, followed by Pippa, Stardust, Diva and Zimb. She knew the Cloud Forest like the back of her hoof and led the group on a twisty route through the tall trees and hidden tunnels in between the vines and bushes.

'Thanks, Harmony. We'd never have found our way out so quickly,' Pippa said, blinking as they finally emerged from the forest.

'I'll lead from here,' offered Zimb. He hovered at head height so that everyone could follow him.

Pippa's heartbeat matched the pounding of Stardust's hooves as they sped over the rugged ground. 'Faster,' she urged, loving the feel of the wind in her face and her hair streaming behind her.

They galloped around the base of the Volcano and finally Zimb slowed down to let everyone catch their breath. As they continued their journey the ground grew steeper. Soon the ponies' coats

were speckled with sweat and their sides were heaving again.

'How much further?' gasped Stardust.

'We're nearly there,' said Zimb, as they approached the top of a ridge. 'The cavesss are down there.'

Pippa's stomach lurched as she looked down at the craggy cliff face and a large, bowl-shaped cove below. She'd mostly overcome her fear of heights but she still didn't like them. *Be brave*, she told herself. Then she caught a sound on the breeze and her pinched face cleared. 'I can hear someone laughing,' she said.

'It must be Divine!' exclaimed Diva. 'Quick – how do we get to the beach?'

'The path isss there,' Zimb said, flying towards it. 'Careful, it's narrow.'

Zimb wasn't exaggerating, thought Pippa as Stardust picked her way down the winding cliff path. In some places it was only just wide enough for one hoof at a time. Pippa stared ahead and tried not to think about the sheer drop to the side. She was breathless with relief when Stardust finally stepped on to the soft sand of the beach.

'The entrance to the cavesss isss over there . . .' Zimb broke off, staring across the beach in dismay. 'But the tide is coming in. Unless you can fly like me, you won't be able to reach it.'

Pippa stared at the massive, dome-shaped cave. It was even larger than the cathedral not far from where she lived. 'How high does the water come up when the tide's in?' she asked.

'About halfway,' said Zimb. 'The tunnelsss flood at high tide. It'sss not sssafe for you to enter without a boat.'

Pippa fell silent as her eyes scanned the beach for driftwood. If they could find enough they could build a raft. But that was a crazy idea. Even with wood how could they make a raft without any tools?

Harmony sighed. 'There's no way in,' she said, wishing that her horn had the power to freeze water like some unicorns could.

'Maybe there is,' said Diva. She walked in a circle, kicking up the sand with her hooves. 'There!'

Triumphantly, Diva reached down and plucked a horn-shaped conch shell from the beach. The shell gleamed in the sunlight. Diva shook the sand from inside it. She lifted it to her lips and blew softly into the end. A long, deep note filled the air. Diva kept blowing until the cove seemed to shake with the mellow sound.

'Look,' shouted Stardust.

Sailing around the rocks at the mouth of the cove was an enormous boat with three masts, purple and gold sails and cannons lining the decks. Pippa stared at the top of the tallest mast. It was sporting a small, black triangular sail. Her mouth opened in surprise. 'Look, a horseshoe and crossbones!'

'Pirate ponies,' Diva said, smugly, tossing her head. 'They're some of my biggest fans.'

As the boat sailed closer a chunky black and white horse with a cropped mane, wearing a pirate's hat and a purple eyepatch over his left eye, came and stood at the bows. 'Aaargh!' he said. 'Ahoy there, me hearties. Who did call for the swashbucklin' pirate ponies?'

'Pieces of eight, eight pieces,' shrieked a blue and red parrot, perched on the Captain's shoulder.

'Shall I fire the cannon, sir?' A chestnut pony with a blonde mane and tail muscled her way over to the Captain.

'Don't ye be doin' that,' said the Captain. 'If I'm not mistaken, there be me favourite singer, the talented Diva. We were just on our way to your concert, lassie. Has the venue changed then?'

'The concert is still at Stableside Castle, but there's been a hitch.' Pippa quickly explained to the Captain and his pirate crew how Divine had stolen Diva's voice. 'So we need to sail into the caves,' she finished. 'Please, can you take us there on your ship?'

'Aye, Captain Rascal and the crew of the good ship *The Jolly Horseshoe* are happy to sail anywhere you ask,' said Captain Rascal, 'and all for the price of a song.'

Diva paled. 'A song?'

'Aye. "A Pirate's Life for Me". It's me favourite pirate sea shanty.'

'Oh! I think I know that one. It goes like this — *Yo! It's a pirate's life for me . . .*' Diva trailed off when she realised everyone was looking at her.

'*Yo!*' Pippa shouted, enthusiastically. 'Join in everyone. *It's a pirate's life for me.*'

'*Sailing the glistening sea.*
Pirate ponies have all the fun.
While landlubbing ponies get none!
Hey!'

Pippa glanced at Diva as she sang. The pony was singing quietly so that Pippa had to strain her ears to hear.

She leaned across and whispered in Diva's ear, 'You have a beautiful voice.'

Diva turned as red as an apple. 'Really? You're not just saying that? Only this is my speaking voice, not my proper singing one.'

'Really,' Pippa said, firmly. If she could convince Diva that all she needed was some self-confidence then it wouldn't matter if they failed to get Diva's proper singing voice back in time for the concert.

'Bravo!' boomed Captain Rascal. 'That was as lovely as a sunset at sea! Come aboard, me hearties, and I'll sail you where ye need to be.'

Led by Zimb, the ponies and Harmony waded out to the pirate ship. Two girl pirates, wearing matching polka dot bandanas, lowered a gangplank and they scrambled aboard. The crew adjusted the sails, leaving a small one flying at the front, and the boat glided slowly into the caves. Inside it was so black that Pippa couldn't even see her hand when she held it in front of her face. She shivered and wrapped her arms around her chest.

'What's that noise?' whispered Stardust.

At first Pippa could only hear the steady drip of water on rock. She pushed her hair away from her ears and then she heard it too. 'It's Divine and it sounds like she's singing,' she whispered back.

'That's so spooky,' Diva said, sounding perplexed. 'I hope she's not going to use my voice next.'

'Don't worry.' Pippa reached out and stroked Diva's neck. 'I promise we'll get your singing voice back soon.'

Chapter 5

The pirate ship creaked then shuddered to a halt.

'Here we are. Away ye go, me hearties,' boomed Captain Rascal.

'Away ye go,' echoed the parrot.

Pippa leaned forward but even when she scrunched her eyes up she couldn't see a thing. How the Captain knew they'd arrived at the entrance to the tunnels was a mystery to her.

'Where do we get off the boat?' she asked.

'Over there,' replied a friendly voice. A light shone behind her. Pippa turned and saw one of the polka dot pirates carrying a lantern attached to a long pole. 'Here, take this,' said the pirate pony.

'Thanks,' said Pippa. In the light she could see that the tunnel ceiling was quite low so she slipped from Stardust's back. The pirates had lowered the gangplank and it was resting on a rock. Pippa went over and held the light so that Stardust, followed by Diva and Harmony, could see to get off the boat. When it was Pippa's turn the plank creaked as she placed her foot on it. Pippa stood very still. She gripped the lantern tightly as she plucked up the courage to walk the plank. 'At least there aren't any sharks,' she told herself firmly. But who knew what else was lurking down in the oil-black seawater beneath her!

Halfway across the plank Pippa heard a splash. She froze. What was that? The water was still again but Pippa was stuck. The plank seemed to go on for ever. Would she really make it to the end without falling off?

'Come on, Pippa, you're nearly there now,' called Stardust encouragingly.

'You can do it,' said Diva. 'We know you can!'

Pippa took a deep breath. Of course she could do it if she believed in herself. Isn't that what she'd been telling Diva? Pippa smiled at Stardust and her cousin. 'I can,' she said, loudly, and she took another step.

Once she got going again, it was easy. Pippa practically ran the last few steps and jumped off the plank. The lantern flickered and she steadied it with her free hand. 'Whoops! Mustn't let it go out,' she said. 'Then we will be stuck!'

The moment everyone stepped ashore the pirates raised the gangplank.

'Aren't you coming with us?' asked Pippa.

'Nay. We're pirate ponies, not landlubbers. We belong at sea,' said Captain Rascal. 'Good luck, me heart-ies.'

The tunnel was only wide enough for everyone to walk in single file. Pippa had to go first as she was carrying the lantern but Zimb flew by her shoulder. Water trickled down the rocky walls and made puddles on the ground. Barnacles and mussels clung to the rocks, their shells clamped tightly together. The tunnel twisted and turned. In some places it was so low that everyone had to bow their heads to avoid scraping them on the rocky ceiling.

Pippa couldn't stop shivering but Zimb's soft voice, whispering in her ear, gave her the courage to go on. Often the tunnel split and sometimes there were multiple passages to choose from. Then Diva would stand with her ears pricked until she picked up the sound of Divine's voice drifting towards her. They walked for ages. One of Pippa's shoes was beginning to rub the back of her ankle when suddenly the tunnel opened out into a small, rocky cave littered with slimy seaweed.

'There she is!' Pippa pointed to the middle of the cave where Divine stood with her back to them. A glass bottle was propped between her front hooves. Her nose was in the air and her mouth wide open as she sang gustily to the empty cave.

'My voice!' cried Diva. Her eyes were bright with tears as she stared round at her friends. 'She's got my voice in that bottle!'

Divine stopped singing and swung round. 'It's *my* voice now,' she crowed.

Pippa clenched her hands. 'It's not. That's Diva's singing voice and you stole it.'

Divine cackled with laughter. 'You again! You don't give up, do you?'

'No, I don't,' Pippa said, bravely. *Yes, you do,* said a small voice in her head. *Remember rehearsing the play with Miranda? You gave up then, didn't you?* Pippa felt hot inside but she squashed the thought flat and turned her attention back to Divine. 'Now give Diva her voice back or –'

'Or what?' Divine said, scornfully. 'You'll run and tell your mummykins? Too late, foolish child. I shall sing at the concert tonight and everyone will love *me*.'

Love me ... love me ... love me ... Divine's voice echoed softly in the cave.

71

'Give me the bottle, please.' Pippa stepped towards Divine. 'You've made Diva very upset.'

'Stay back!' Divine raised a hoof in warning. 'Come any closer and I'll smash this bottle on the rocks. Then Diva's precious voice will be lost for ever.'

For ever . . . for ever . . . for ever . . . called the echo.

Pippa froze. She was convinced that Diva didn't need her singing voice back to be able to sing again – all she needed was to believe that she could do it. But what if she were wrong? She couldn't take that risk.

'Zimb,' Pippa said in a low voice. 'Can you sneak round her and get the bottle?'

'I shall try,' he replied.

On silent wings, Zimb flew over to Divine.

'Divine,' Pippa called, hoping to distract her. 'You don't need someone else's voice to be loved. If you treat the other ponies nicely and show them how much you love them then everyone will want to be your friend.'

Divine's eyes flashed hopefully. 'Why should I believe you?'

'Because —' Pippa started but it was too late. Zimb had reached the bottle and snatched it from the floor.

Divine wheeled round. 'Little thief!' she squealed.

Thief . . . thief . . . thief . . . the cave called back.

'That's it, Zimb!' said Pippa.

Zimb was struggling. The bottle was too heavy for him to carry. When Divine's flaying hooves knocked the bottle, Zimb let go. Pippa went cold with fear as it sailed through the air. She jumped to save it but the jar slipped through her fingers. There was a fierce crack as it hit the rocks and broke apart. Shards of glass pinged around the cave and Pippa covered her head with her hands to protect herself. A long silence followed. As Pippa uncurled her hands from her head a low moan filled the cave.

'Nooooo,' wailed Diva. 'My singing voice . . . it's lost for ever.'

'Ha, ha, ha!' Divine squinted, making her eyes look small and mean. 'Serves you right for meddling. If I can't have your voice, no one can.' Swirling her cloak around her she leapt into a tunnel at the back of the cave and galloped away.

Pippa listened to her hooves echoing into the distance. 'I'm sorry.' She threw her arms around Diva's black neck. 'I'm so very sorry.'

'I used to be special – now I'm just ordinary.' Diva's sobs rang around the cave. 'I'll never sing again. Never!'

Something was tickling Pippa's ankles. She stamped her feet and felt water splash up her legs. Fearfully, she glanced down. 'Oh no!' she cried. 'We've been here too long. The tide's coming in.'

'It's over my hooves already,' squeaked Stardust. 'Help! What are we going to do?'

Chapter 6

Pippa's head spun. They were going to be trapped in the watery tunnels.

'I'll fly to Stableside Castle for help,' said Zimb.

'There isn't time,' said Pippa. 'We'll have to call for the pirates.'

Stardust looked worried. 'But they'll never hear us in here. We don't have the conch shell to make our voices louder.'

'Diva has a powerful voice,' said Harmony. 'The pirates would hear her . . . if she sang.'

Diva shook her head. 'I'm sorry but I can't do it,' she said, dramatically.

'We're all here for you,' said Pippa, stroking Diva's flowing mane. 'We believe in you.'

As she waited for Diva to reply, Pippa crossed her fingers. If Diva said yes then she would try harder at all the things she found difficult too, starting with her lines for the play.

'Oh, OK,' Diva said, reluctantly. 'I'll try.'

'That's my Diva,' said Harmony.

'Ssstand back, give Diva some room,' instructed Zimb.

Diva stood alone in the centre of the cave. Pippa held the lantern out to make a spotlight. There was a faraway look in Diva's eyes as she opened her mouth and began to sing. '*Yo! It's a pirate's life for me . . .*' she crooned.

'That's so beautiful,' called Pippa. 'Again, Diva. Louder this time.'

Diva blushed. 'Thank you, Pippa,' she said. '*YO! IT'S A PIRATE'S LIFE FOR ME*,' she began again.

As Diva sang the pirate sea shanty, the echo sang it back to her. Pippa swallowed a lump in her throat. She'd never heard such a wonderful voice. Zimb ushered everyone along the tunnel, back to the cave where the pirate ship had left them. The water was rising too quickly. By the time they reached the cave it was up to Pippa's knees. She held the lantern high above her head and peered into the gloom. Where was *The Jolly Horseshoe*?

Suddenly Diva stopped singing, but her voice continued to echo through the tunnels.

Diva's ears swivelled forward. 'Is that what I sound like?' she asked.

'You sound like a star,' said Pippa.

'With an audience,' added Stardust. 'Look!'

Pippa looked to the mouth of the cave just in time to see *The Jolly Horseshoe* sail through. 'Hoorah!' she cheered. 'You did it, Diva. You haven't lost your singing voice at all. There was no magic in that potion! Divine stole something else from you, something much more important – your confidence.'

Diva stared at Pippa with a mixture of surprise and joy. 'You're right, Pippa. I can sing. But it's not too late, is it? I haven't missed the concert?'

'No,' said Pippa, as the thud of *The Jolly Horseshoe*'s gangplank echoed around the cave. 'There's still time to get you back to Stableside Castle for your performance.'

Captain Rascal insisted on sailing everyone around the coast to the beach nearest to Stableside Castle. 'It's a pirate's life for us,' he laughed.

'There won't be enough time to get you ready.' Stardust fussed over Diva. 'And we've missed our appointment at the Mane Street Salon. Can any of you pirate ponies please lend me a brush so that I can try and smarten Diva up a bit?'

Stardust's request was met with gales of laughter. 'A brush!' The pirates with the spotty bandanas giggled. 'What's a brush?'

'Don't worry, Stardust,' said Diva. 'I don't mind how I look. It's more important that I give my best when I'm singing.'

Pippa smiled to herself. Diva wasn't the diva she'd seemed when they first met. 'That's true,' she said. 'But Stardust has a point. You're a star, Diva, and the Royal Ponies will expect you to look tidy.'

Pippa used her fingers to untangle the worst knots in Diva's mane and tail. She found a clean tissue in her pocket and wiped the mud from the Cloud Forest away from Diva's face. 'You look great,' she said, stepping back to admire her work.

The strong wind blew the boat around the island. It wasn't long before *The Jolly Horseshoe* arrived at the beach where Rosella had left Pippa. 'Not far now,' said Pippa. 'Are you ready to sing, Diva?'

'I'm readier than I've ever been,' Diva said, with a smile.

There was a loud rattle and the boat

shook as Captain Rascal dropped the anchor. 'All landlubbers ashore,' he cried, lowering the plank.

'Aren't you coming with us?' asked Stardust.

'Not me. I'm staying aboard for the finale.'

'The finale?' Stardust was mystified.

Captain Rascal winked. 'Let's just say that I'm here to make sure the evening ends with a bang.'

As Pippa, Stardust, Diva, Harmony and Zimb made their way to Stableside Castle they were joined by some of Zimb's horsefly friends. 'We came to sssee where you were,' they buzzed. 'The unicornsss are here too. They're already ssseated in the amphitheatre next to the ponies from the Mighty Oaksss Senior Ponies Stables, who didn't get to hear the concert earlier.'

As the turrets of the Castle grew nearer Pippa felt fizzy with excitement. Diva was very quiet but her face was set with determination.

'You're going to be brilliant,' Pippa whispered.

'I'll give it my best,' Diva replied.

The amphitheatre was buzzing with chatter as Pippa and Stardust took their seats in the royal box.

Queen Moonshine leaned forward in her seat. 'We were beginning to worry that you wouldn't make it,' she whinnied.

'Did Divine give Diva her singing voice back?' asked Princess Crystal. 'Is it as good as it was?'

'Wait and see,' Stardust said, with a smile.

'What about Diva's hooves and mane and tail? Did she get them done? Only she missed her appointment at the

Mane Street Salon,' Princess Honey said, anxiously.

Before Pippa or Stardust could answer the conductor tapped his baton against his music stand. The audience fell silent. A soft, pink spotlight circled the stage and came to rest in the centre where Diva stood with her head bowed. Bathed in light, she turned to the royal box and curtsied to the King and Queen. She winked at Pippa and Stardust, then throwing back her head she began to sing.

After the performance the audience went wild. They cheered and stamped their hooves and some threw wild flowers on to the stage. Diva was made to sing three encores before finally the conductor tapped his baton on his music stand for silence. Diva stepped forward. In a low voice she addressed the crowd. 'Ponies, unicorns, Pippa MacDonald and friends of Chevalia, thank you. Your support means so much to me. It was only with the help and love of my friends that I made it here tonight. They taught me a lesson that I'll always remember. Never give up on your dreams. If you believe in yourself then you can make good things happen. I believe in me but I also believe in Chevalia, a magical place for ponies and their friends. To Chevalia.'

'To Chevalia.' As the roar of the crowd died away pink stars exploded overhead.

Pippa stared up as more bangs sounded and the sky was filled with a rainbow of coloured stars. 'Fireworks,' she said, happily.

'So that's what Captain Rascal meant when he said the evening would end with a bang! I love fireworks,' Stardust added.

'Me too,' said Pippa as a rocket whizzed into the night sky and exploded in a myriad of coloured sparkles. 'What a perfect end to a brilliant concert.'

After the concert everyone wanted to congratulate Diva on how well she'd sung. There was such a huge crowd around her that Pippa and Stardust couldn't even see her. Gradually the ponies drifted away. When at last Diva was on her own again she made straight for Pippa and her cousin Stardust. Her eyes shone with happiness. 'Thank you,' Diva said.

'No, thank you,' said Pippa. 'You

showed me how important confidence is. You're a truly extraordinary pony, Diva.'

Stardust neighed. 'Let's get something to eat. The buffet looks delicious and I'm hungry after all that excitement.'

There was plenty of food. Stardust and Diva tucked into carrot burgers and hot popped oats, washing them down with steaming carrot juice. To Pippa's delight the Stableside cook had remembered her too. She had her own dish of fish and chips served in a paper box and a mug of hot chocolate. Pippa drained the hot chocolate and licked her lips. 'How come food tastes so much better when it's eaten outdoors?' she asked.

'I don't know but it does!' Princess Stardust agreed.

'Sssorry to break up the party.' Zimb hovered by Pippa's ear. 'Captain Rascal is ready to take you home, Pippa.'

'I'm sailing home on a pirate ship!' Pippa's face lit up.

'Can I come too?' asked Stardust.

'Of courssse,' said Zimb. 'Go and sssay your goodbyes, Pippa.'

There was a heavy feeling in Pippa's chest as she said goodbye to her friends. She didn't want to leave, but she knew it was time to return home and practise for the school play.

'You're always welcome in Chevalia,' said Queen Moonshine, as Pippa curtsied. 'We hope to see you soon.'

Pippa flushed. She hoped to be back soon. Chevalia was her special place.

The pirate ponies sang sea shanties and told tall tales of their adventures on the high seas. Pippa decided to practise for the school play. She stood on the deck and recited her lines, pretending to be a brave knight. The pirates applauded her and asked for more.

'For the price of a song,' Pippa replied, with a smile.

They sang more sea shanties all the way home. Pippa and Stardust joined in and the journey passed even more quickly than usual. Pippa could hardly believe it when *The Jolly Horseshoe* pulled up on the riverbank, alongside the bulrushes where she'd first seen Rosella.

'Goodbye, Stardust.' Pippa gave the pony the longest hug ever.

'Goodbye, Pippa. See you soon?'

'I'm sure of it,' said Pippa, as she hopped on to the bank. She turned to wave goodbye but *The Jolly Horseshoe* had gone. Pippa stared at the empty river for a long moment, then she took a deep breath. The adventure wasn't

quite over. There was one thing left to do. She strode over to the tree where Miranda was reading her book.

Pippa cleared her throat. 'I've changed my mind,' she said, confidently. 'I'm going to practise my play now. Please will you be my audience?'

'All right, Pippa,' said Miranda, with a smile. She put her book down. 'Are you ready to be a star?'

Pippa smiled back and stood tall. She was ready.

LIVE IN CONCERT

DIVA

Duchess of Savannah

Singing her No. 1 songs: *Jump That Bar* & *Midnight Ride*

Accompanied
by the
**Royal Pony
Orchestra**

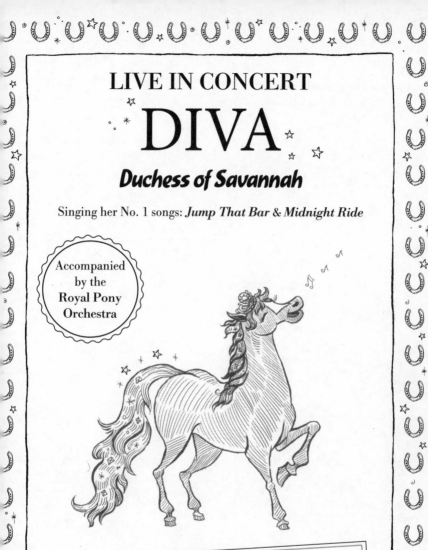

 TONIGHT
at Stableside Castle

Concert begins at sunset. No ponies will be seated after Diva starts.

Chevalia Now!

EXCLUSIVE INTERVIEW WITH DIVA

Chevalia's singing superstar!

By Tulip Inkhoof

1

After a sensational performance at what is being called Stableside Castle's concert of the year, this reporter was granted a backstage interview with superstar, Diva, to talk about what really went on behind the scenes in the lead-up to the show.

☆ **TI (Tulip Inkhoof):** First of all, Diva, let me just say: I'm a big fan.

☆ **D (Diva):** No you're not, you're a pony! Ha ha ha! Seriously, though, Tunic –

☆ **TI:** It's Tulip, actually.

☆ **D:** How lovely for you, *da . . . ha . . . ling*. As I was saying, of course you're a fan. Foals look up to me and ponies want to be me. I'm Diva, the Duchess of Savannah!

☆ **TI:** You're sure of yourself, aren't you?

☆ **D:** Why yes! If I don't believe in myself, then neither will my fans.

☆ **TI:** Can you tell our readers where all of that confidence comes from?

☆ **D:** When I'm singing, it's just me out there on stage, in front of thousands of cheering ponies. To give them what they want and what they expect, I have to be the best. I dig deep, right down to my horseshoes, and summon up all my courage and confidence. Tunis, I'll let you in on a little secret . . .

☆ **TI:** It's Tulip, Tulip Inkhoof, and that'd be great.

☆ **D:** As a foal I wasn't the best singer in Savannah, and along the way I've faced plenty of rejection. I remember wanting to sing so badly that my mare took me to the Winter Fair to try out for the Chevalia Choir. I hadn't prepared and I was awful. Everyone laughed at me.

☆ **TI:** How terrible!

4

D: I never forgot that day, and ever since then I've always rehearsed and prepared. Even when I'm the star attraction at a big concert, I still feel just one gallop away from that little foal who messed up her first audition. That's where confidence comes in. It gets me over that jump – no matter how high it is.

TI: That's very inspiring. Can you tell our readers what happened to your singing voice before the concert tonight?

Chevalia was rife with rumours that you'd lost your voice. There was even talk of dark magic afoot.

✩ **D:** That sneaky pony Divine convinced me she'd used a potion to take my voice – and I fell for it. But it was my confidence that I lost! I got caught up in my own fame and thought that it was just my voice that made me who I am. Now I know that's not true.

✩ **TI:** Well, your voice *is* wonderful. We hear that the infamous pirate Captain Rascal

6

thinks so too. Is he the fearless thief that the ponarazzi report him to be?

D: Not in the least! After all, he helped me to find my most precious treasure: my confidence.

Dear Stardust,

I'm going to give this letter to the seahorses to take to you. I do hope that it reaches you.

I'm back at school now. Chevalia seems so far away, and yet you, and all of the other ponies, are in my heart.

Yesterday was the school play. I practised and rehearsed all week, and when I stepped on to the stage, dressed up as a brave knight, I delivered my lines loudly without forgetting even one.

9

Mum said I looked like a natural up there, especially when I rode my loyal 'horse' – which was actually two boys from my class dressed up in a horse costume! You would have laughed so hard.

I can't believe that just a week ago I was too timid to perform in front of an audience. I was scared that everyone would laugh at me.

But after everything we've been through on Chevalia, I knew that I was silly to feel so afraid. If there's one thing I have learned during our adventures together, it's that I can do anything! Whether you know it or not, Stardust, you taught me that.

I hope to see you very soon. I miss you and everyone on the island (well, not Divine).

11

Mum says she'll take me to a horse show, but it's not the same. I'll see you in my dreams!

Love,
Pippa MacDonald

PS – Oh, I've included a copy of the poster for the school play!

Burlington Middle School
proudly presents

KNIGHTS OF THE ROUND TABLE

FEATURING

PIPPA MACDONALD as the Brave Knight

DAVID TOMLINSON & MARCUS O'REILLY as her Horse

IYLA NORTON as Jasper

Knights of the Round Table is an epic tale of bravery
and courage, written by Ms Markin's students,
based on the stories of King Arthur.

The play begins at 7.30 p.m.
No parents will be seated after the performance starts.